Tafari
The Special Child

BEVERLEY WILSON

ISBN: 1977699863
ISBN-13: 9781977699862

A long time ago in Ethiopia, there lived a good nobleman named Ras Makonnen. He was as brave as a knight. He was wiser than all the emperor's men, and he was kind.

One day, Ras Makonnen met a beautiful and charming young lady, and they got married. Her name was Wayzaro Yashimabet.

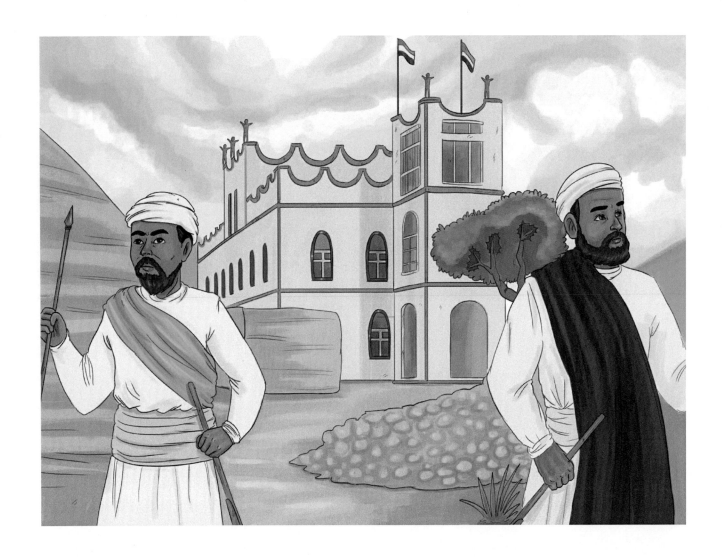

Many years later, Ras Makonnen and Wayzaro Yashimabet lived in a lovely palace, but they had no children. Unfortunately, they had lost one, two, three, four, five, six, seven, eight, then nine precious children! So, they prayed every day for a healthy and beautiful child.

Early one morning, Ras Makonnen sat alone in his church. He was very worried, so he told the priest his problem.

"My wife and I are longing to have a child, but we have been very unlucky."

"Don't worry," said the priest. " Keep praying, and God will show you his Wonderful Goodness!"

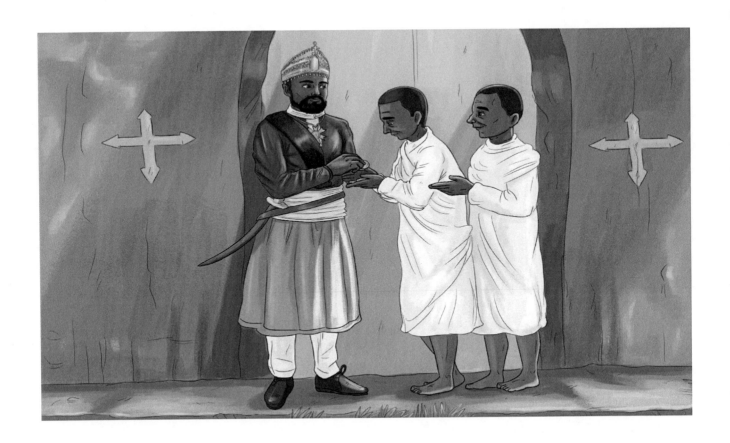

On his way home that day, Ras Makonnen met some poor and hungry beggars.

"Your Highness! Please, can we have some food?" asked one of the beggars, as he reached out to touch Ras Makonnen's arm.

Ras Makonnen gave them money to buy bread and honey.

"Thank you, Your Highness!" they cried cheerfully. "May the Almighty bless you!"

In the whole of Ethiopia, everyone was fond of Ras Makonnen, especially the people in Harar. Inside the town were Ras Makonnen's palace and a very busy market, where people came to buy and sell.

"**Myrrh, frankincense, coffee, flour**, and **corn!**" shouted the people.

At the palace, Wayzaro Yashimabet strolled around her beautiful garden. Ras Makonnen would soon be home. She had a wonderful surprise to tell him.

Later, in the evening, Wayzaro Yashimabet told Ras Makonnen the wonderful surprise. "I'm going to have a baby!" she said excitedly.

They were both very happy. However, when the servants heard the news, they were worried.

"Wayzaro Yashimabet is going to have another child."

"Oh! No! Will this child live?"

Long before the baby was born, there was a terrible drought. The rain did not fall, and the sun baked the ground like a blazing oven. The crops did not grow. There was no food to eat, and no water to drink.

But one day in the month of July, it looked as if the rain would fall.

Suddenly, it became very dark like it was in the middle of the night.

During the night, the dark, dark sky was lit up with flashes of lightning like shooting stars. **Boom! Boom! Boom!** The sound of thunder rumbled and grumbled and shook the earth. The wind hummed gently, "Rain, rain, come down now. Rain, rain, come down now."

Pitter-patter, pitter-patter, pitter-patter - so came the rain as it started falling from the clouds. It fell lightly at first - drip drop, drip drop, drip drop. Then it fell heavily on the trees and the ground.

The faithful moon peeped out from behind the clouds. Something wonderful was happening that night.

The rain fell everywhere. It poured down on a small, round hut in the little village of Ejarsa Gora. Wayzaro Yashimabet had gone there to have her baby. While she waited, the villagers prayed. Priests chanted, and the smell of frankincense filled the air.

On that stormy night, while lightning flashed and thunder clapped, a beautiful baby boy was born. That was on 23 July 1892. "Waah! Waah! Waah!" cried the baby.

"God has been good to us," said Ras Makonnen. "He has given us a beautiful and healthy son." They called him Tafari. Tafari is a name that means "to be respected or feared."

Forty days after Tafari was born, it was time for his special baptism. The priest filled his shiny **gold** censer with **frankincense** and **myrrh**. He blessed Tafari and gave him a special name. Only his parents and the priest knew his baptismal name, so it became his secret name.

After Tafari was born, Mother Nature blessed the land. There was plenty of food to eat and lots of water to drink. Everyone was happy, and Wayzaro Yashimabet was full of joy!

A King is Crowned

Tafari grew up in his father's palace, and there, he followed close behind his mother until the night she disappeared before he was two years old. He was waiting to feel her warm, loving arms wrapped around him, but he never felt them again. After a while, he couldn't remember her anymore.

When Tafari was old enough, he went to school at the palace with his cousin, Imru. The two of them were like twins, and their favourite teacher was Abba Samuel. Abba Samuel told his father, "I am delighted to teach Tafari. I've never met such an intelligent child!"

" He was born to be a king," said Ras Makonnen. "I'm glad he came to us on that stormy night. He's a gift from God."

As Tafari grew older, many astonishing stories were told about him. Once, after he was accused of hitting a boy in his forehead with a stone, he whispered in the young boy's ear. Suddenly, the boy raised his head and pointed to another boy, who had thrown the stone, before closing his eyes again. And when he drew a picture of a bird, it flew out of the paper, just like a magician's trick.

Soon, everyone was enchanted by Tafari. He was as wise as a king, and his deep dark eyes were as mysterious as the stars. At school, he was only ever in trouble for studying too much! When his lessons were over, he went back to his classroom to learn some more.

One marvellous day, Ras Makonnen found Tafari in his palace, speaking to: doctors, priests and powerful men.

"Oh, what a clever son you have!" said a rich man to Ras Makonnen.

But the horrible men, rushed out of the palace when Tafari gazed into their cruel eyes. He knew who was good and who was evil.

No one was surprised when his father made him chief of Gara Muleta.

Suddenly, on a gloomy day, everyone was sad. The emperor wept. The people wailed, and Tafari's tears ran down his nose and down his cheeks.

"It won't ever feel the same again without my father," he sobbed to his grandmother. "I loved him dearly, with all of my heart."

Poor Tafari! He was now an orphan, and his secret name was buried like a treasure in a chest. Off he went with his cousin Imru to live at the Imperial Palace with the old and wise emperor, who was called Menelik II. He adored Tafari and kept him close by his side.

The nobles at Menelik's court were very excited when Tafari arrived. He spoke French, English, Amharic and Geez. "Isn't he amazing!" they cried.

Then the same nobles became curious. "He's different!" said a nobleman. "He's not like an ordinary child. He only wants to study. Ha! Ha! Ha!" he laughed out loud.

Inside the palace, the mean and jealous noblemen were frustrated. They couldn't get Tafari to join them, to get rid of the emperor. They whispered behind his back.

"This is no place for a smart child, especially Ras Makonnen's son. If he stays here, he will want to become the emperor."

"Don't worry," said the other man. "I have a plan to make sure that Lij Iyasu, becomes the next emperor."

Unfortunately, Tafari had to leave the emperor and the palace. He had to go on a long journey. With his men, he travelled to far away towns and became their leader. He was as brave as a lion, charming as a prince, and kind like his father.

When Tafari grew up, he married a beautiful, kind lady called Wayzaro Menen. They lived happily together in Harar until there was trouble at the Emperor's palace.

Lij Iyasu was the new emperor, but he was behaving rather badly. They didn't crown him. So, the good noblemen went to find a wise young man. "Will you be our prince?" they asked Tafari.

Tafari refused. He was confused. He pondered. Eventually, he agreed. He became the Crown Prince of Ethiopia, and he was given the title Ras, which means Head. Tafari was now called **Ras Tafari!**

Many years later, Tafari, was crowned a second time. This time he was crowned **Negus**! Negus means king.

On the **second of November 1930**, Tafari (*King Ras Tafari*) was crowned for the third time in St George's Cathedral.

Abuna Kyrillos, the chief priest, put a golden crown on Tafari's head. Then, he called him, "**Haile Selassie I...**" That was Tafari's secret name! Now, everyone knew the name Haile Selassie I. It was no longer hidden. It is an Ethiopian name. In English, the name means **Power of the Trinity**, TAFARI-RASTAFARI-HAILE SELASSIE I.

Wayzaro Menen was also crowned. She became the Empress of Ethiopia.

After the coronation, the new emperor invited everyone to a splendid feast. He had triumphed to become emperor. As he sat happily on his throne with his family, he watched the Ethiopian people celebrate for many days and nights.

So, **Tafari** was the special child who became the Emperor of Ethiopia, **His Imperial Majesty**, **Haile Selassie I**, **Conquering Lion of the Tribe of Judah, king of kings, Elect of God,** and he ruled his people wisely for many, many years.

About the Author

After spending a number of years researching the early childhood and life of one of Ethiopia's greatest emperors, His Imperial Majesty, Emperor Haile Selassie I, Beverley felt compelled to tell the story. She became fascinated by the mysterious, intriguing circumstances surrounding his birth and his rise to the throne. She knew that this story had all the ingredients of a wonderful tale that could captivate young readers. Initially, she told the story orally to young children and was encouraged by their responses. Currently, Beverley works as a Primary Education Consultant, and before that, she worked in education for more than twenty years. She clearly understands the power of telling a good story, and the use of imagery to engage the reader. She is keen to point out that this is her first book, and even though the story is written imaginatively, it is largely based on factual information.

71404224R00018

Made in the USA
San Bernardino, CA
15 March 2018